964

William B. Eerdmans Publishing Company
Grand Rapids, Michigan

CARLOS
© Copyright 1986 by Scandinavia
Publishing House, Nørregade 32, DK-1165 Copenhagen K.
English language edition first published 1987
through special arrangement with Scandinavia
by W. B. Eerdmans Publishing Co.,
255 Jefferson Ave. S.E. Grand Rapids, Michigan 49503

Printed in Singapore

ISBN 0-8028-5019-7

I would like to thank Joseph C.
Rast III for his good work in
assisting photographer Ben
Alex on assignment in Brazil.
 The character of Tia Noeme is
not fictional. Her work is very
much like that shown in this
book. She is the director of an
organization that provides
assistance to abandoned
children in São Paulo.
Contributions to her ministry
may be sent to:
Associaçao Tia Noeme
e Seus Amiguinhos
Caixa Postal 54016
CEP 01296 São Paulo, SP
Brazil

         Marcos Carpenter

CARLOS
The Street Boy Who Found a Home

Marcos Carpenter

Photos by Ben Alex

964

William B. Eerdmans Publishing Company
Grand Rapids, Michigan

It was late afternoon in São Paulo, Brazil's largest city. Rush-hour traffic inched along, bumper to bumper. Carlos was already at the busy intersection where he sold flowers every afternoon.

When the traffic light turned red, Carlos went from car to car. He showed the flowers and offered them at a cheap price. if he didn't hurry out of the way when the light turned green though, he would get run over. It was a dangerous job, and Carlos hated it. But if he didn't earn a pocketful of cash each day, he and his Uncle Bento would go hungry.

"Get out of here!" yelled an angry driver. "Go home!" But Carlos had no home. At night he slept in a tiny shack in one of São Paulo's slums, called **favelas**. Sometimes his Uncle Bento slept there, too, when he was not out drinking.

It was almost dark when Carlos sold the last bunch of roses. With the money safe in his pocket, he started across the park toward the favela where he lived. But Carlos did not look forward to getting back. It was late, and Uncle Bento would be angry that he had had to wait so long before he could go to the bar.

"Where's the money?" Uncle Bento demanded when Carlos came back. Carlos reached deep into his pocket, then held out the small handful of **cruzado**, Brazilian bills. Uncle Bento snatched them away and left the shack. He needed Carlos' money to buy liquor.

For supper, Carlos found some stale scraps of leftover **mandioca**, a starchy white root that tastes like potatoes when cooked. Then he laid a blanket on the bed, and slumped down alongside Uncle Bento's empty bottles.

"If only mother hadn't died," Carlos thought to himself. "If only my father had never gone off and left us. But now he is dead, too." That night Carlos dreamed that his parents were still alive.

When Carlos awoke early the next morning, he found himself lying on the floor covered by a dirty blanket. Uncle Bento was snoring on the bed beside him. Another empty bottle of sugar-cane liquor lay on the floor.

Carlos got up, stretched his sore back, and put on the same ragged clothes he had worn the day before. He took the last piece of dry bread, then decided to go downtown where he could beg some more food. He would not have to be back until the middle of the afternoon, when his uncle arrived with more flowers for him to sell.

Carlos went to the subway station and rode down the escalator. But he had no money for a ticket. When no one was looking, he crawled under the turnstile. Carlos knew it was not honest.

The subway train was crowded with all sorts of people. There was a tall blonde man, several black women, three Asian schoolgirls, and many people with skin like Carlos'. He remembered something he had heard Uncle Bento say: "**O Brasil é de todos nós!** Brazil belongs to the world!" Carlos' uncle had told him most people in Brazil had originally come from other countries all over the world. "That's why there's no such thing as a typical Brazilian," he had said.

The people on the train wore nice clean clothes and looked as though they were going off to important jobs. Across the aisle Carlos spotted a boy his age wearing an expensive running suit and carrying a tennis racket. When the boy saw Carlos looking at him, he stuck his tongue out.

Carlos' face turned red. It seemed as though everyone was staring at his torn clothes and dirty hair. When the subway train made a sharp curve, a young woman lost her balance and leaned against him. Looking with disgust at Carlos, she brushed off her skirt where it had touched him.

Carlos felt as though the entire world hated him.

When the subway train finally pulled into the Praca da Sé station in a large downtown park, Carlos hurried off. He was glad to be away from the glares and stares of all those people. As he came out of the underground station into the sunshine, he forgot about the boy with the tennis racket.

Carlos spotted a group of boys like himself—ragged street kids—playing in the fountain. Carlos jumped in with them. He swam and splashed until an impatient policeman shooed them all away.

There were hundreds of people in the park, hurrying off in different directions. Several crippled people sat on newspapers on the ground, begging for money. "Alms, for the love of God," they pleaded. Other people gathered around street peddlers who sold everything imaginable, including socks, cheap wristwatches, lottery tickets, and stomach medicine. Still others simply sat around, enjoying the sun.

Just then a gang of noisy street kids approached Carlos.

"Hey, look at that man sitting on the bench over there," said one of them. "His wallet is in his shirt pocket. We're going to sneak up behind him and knock him on the head. Then we'll grab the wallet. Want to help? We'll split the money later, OK?"

Carlos wanted the money, but he did not want to hurt the man or rob him. "No. Just leave the guy alone," he exclaimed.

"**Medroso**! Chicken!" they taunted. The boys made fun of Carlos. Then they turned and walked toward the man sitting on the bench.

The man looked up at the gang of boys for just a second, then he went back to reading his newspaper. Suddenly one of the boys dashed around the bench and distracted the man's attention. Another one of the boys snatched his wallet. They ran across the park and disappeared into the crowd.

"I can't believe it!" Carlos said to himself. "They really did it!"

A crowd began to gather. The man pointed straight at Carlos and yelled, "There's one of them! He's one of the thieves!"

Carlos' heart began to beat wildly. "He thinks I did it!" he said out loud. Carlos wanted to run away, but his feet would not move. Suddenly a large hand grabbed the neck of his shirt and nearly lifted him off the ground. A plainclothes policeman! The man pushed him into the back of a van.

Before long, Carlos found himself at the police station. Nothing like this had ever happened to him before. "What are you going to do to me?" he asked. Carlos began to tremble from head to foot. He had heard that street boys were sometimes given beatings at the police headquarters.

"All right, where's the old man's money?" the policeman demanded. He gave Carlos a shove on the shoulder.

"But it wasn't me!" Carlos whimpered. He shrunk back against the wall. After a few more questions Carlos was pushed back into the van and driven away. He was taken to a boys' camp for troublemaking youngsters.

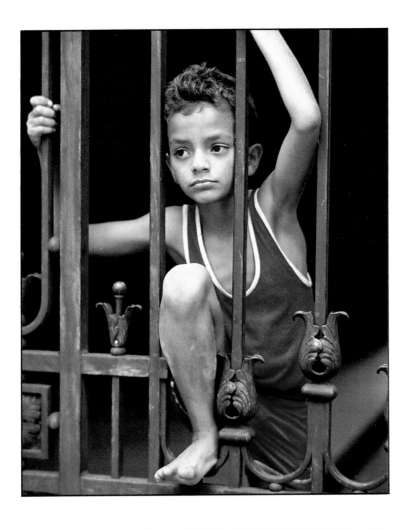

As Carlos walked through the heavy iron gates of the camp, he shuddered with fear. Everyone inside looked tough and mean.

"What'd you do to get sent here?" asked a tall dark boy with a scar on his chest.

"Nothing!" Carlos replied. The boy just laughed at him.

Carlos discovered he was to sleep on a wornout mattress in the same room with at least 80 other boys. He was going to have to sleep right there beside thieves, murderers, and drug pushers. His stomach was in knots.

Three days later, Carlos felt even worse. These street kids did not like him any better than the well-dressed boy on the subway train had. Besides that, a couple of big, tough boys had threatened to beat him up. "You're a coward," they told him. "You won't even admit what you did wrong! You're going to get in trouble with us!"

Later that morning one of the guards announced that a church group from the city would give a puppet show that afternoon. "And if there's any trouble," he warned, "you'll be sorry. I mean it!"

A large group of boys gathered to watch the puppet show. It was led by a pretty woman called Tia Noeme. The boys started to whistle, but most of them listened. When it was over Tia Noeme sang a song for them. She had a lovely voice. To Carlos, she seemed so gentle and caring.

"No matter how bad you've been or how many people you've hurt, Jesus still loves you," she told the boys.

Carlos thought, "Is it possible somebody actually loves me?"

Carlos waited until most of the other boys had left, then he waited, hoping to talk to Tia Noeme. She noticed him coming, and knelt down to meet him.

"What's your name?" she asked, gently drawing him closer.

"Carlos," he whispered, and lowered his head. Suddenly, tears began rolling down his face. Carlos told Tia Noeme everything about the trouble he was in, about his mother who had died when he was four years old, about his dead father, about Uncle Bento, about selling flowers at street corners. He tried to convince her that he had not beat up the man in the park.

Tia Noeme did not laugh at him like the others had. "I'm not sure I can help you get out of here," she said. "But I am sure that Jesus will care for you. He wants you to trust in Him."

Tia Noeme sat down with Carlos and told him more about Jesus. "Jesus is the Son of God," she said. "He came to earth to save people from their sins. We are all sinners."

Carlos remembered all the bad things he had done. He had crawled under the subway turnstile many times without paying. He'd cheated flower-buyers out of their correct change. And sometimes, he had felt hatred toward Uncle Bento.

Tia Noeme broke into Carlos' thoughts. "Jesus will forgive you for everything if you ask Him to. He loves you. Do you want to commit your life to Jesus?"

Carlos did not know what to say. He knew he needed someone stronger than himself to turn to. But something inside him kept saying, "No, no, not now. Not right now."

Tia Noeme understood Carlos' struggle. Right there she bowed her head and prayed, "Lord Jesus, give Carlos the courage to accept You and to trust You."

She turned to Carlos and said, "Remember, you can pray anytime. Just talk to Jesus as if He were your very best friend. And I'll be praying for you, too."

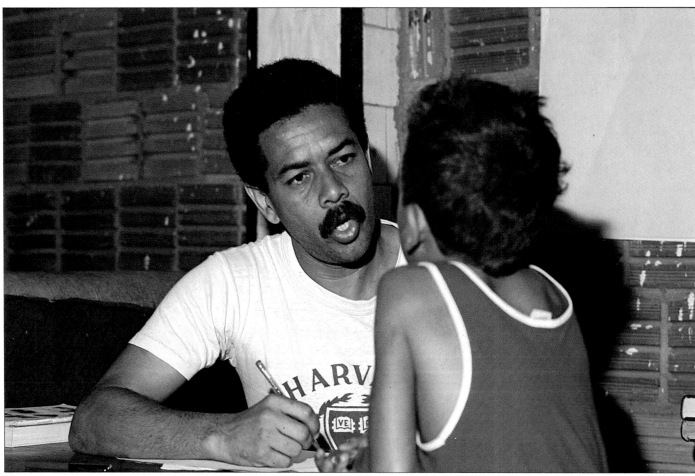

That night as Carlos lay down on the hard mattress alongside all the other boys, he thought about Tia Noeme's prayer. He knew he wanted Jesus. He wished he had prayed while he still had the chance.

He closed his eyes and whispered, "Jesus, I'm all alone. Help me, somehow. Forgive me and help me trust in You."

Then Carlos fell asleep. Little did he know that Someone who loved him was very close . . . as close as his own heart.

"Carlos! **Acorda**! Wake up!"

Carlos sat up straight and rubbed his eyes. It was the early-morning guard shouting in his ear. "Get up!" he repeated. "You got lucky. The man in the park found the real muggers and admitted you were innocent. Those boys will be taking your place here. You're free!"

Carlos could hardly believe his ears. He jumped off the mattress and ran outside. He had to wait at the camp office for an official document to be signed.

The director of the boys' camp looked down at Carlos. "I don't ever want to see you back here," he warned.

"Don't worry," smiled Carlos. "I won't be back!"

Then the iron gate swung open. Carlos was free to go. The air outside seemed cleaner and fresher than before. He started the long walk back to the favela.

By late morning Carlos arrived at the lower entrance of the favela. As he passed through the same old gate, the terrible stench of the open sewers stung his nostrils. He held his nose and started up the hill toward Uncle Bento's shack.

Carlos was not sure what to expect from Uncle Bento. Would he be happy to see Carlos? Would he be angry? Carlos knew if Uncle Bento had been drinking the night before, he would still be sleeping.

As Carlos approached the shack, he noticed the door was open. That meant Uncle Bento was awake. Then an unfamiliar woman appeared in the doorway.

"Where's Uncle Bento?" asked Carlos.

"Who are you?" the lady demanded, her hands on her hips.

Carlos told her who he was.

"Well, listen," she explained, "I don't know why you haven't heard, but your uncle was in a fight last week at the bar. He died of knife wounds. Now this place is mine! And I don't want any kids around! So get out!"

"But what about—" Carlos began. His face was pale.

"I said get out!" the woman screeched.

Carlos stared after the woman as she disappeared back into the shack. Then her words began to sink in. Carlos began walking back down the hill with an aching heart. There was no one else he could go to, and no one he could live with. He felt numb and sick, thinking about Uncle Bento.

"Now what will I do?" he wondered. "I have no money, no place to sleep, no way to get flowers to sell. Why? Why?" The questions tumbled through his mind. He walked and walked, remembering Tia Noeme and the promise she had made to pray for him. Wasn't Jesus supposed to help him? Carlos didn't understand why Jesus had allowed him to be poor and homeless and hungry.

"I just want to be an ordinary kid," he said to himself, choking back tears, "a kid with a mom or a dad, or maybe even both, and all of us with enough to eat."

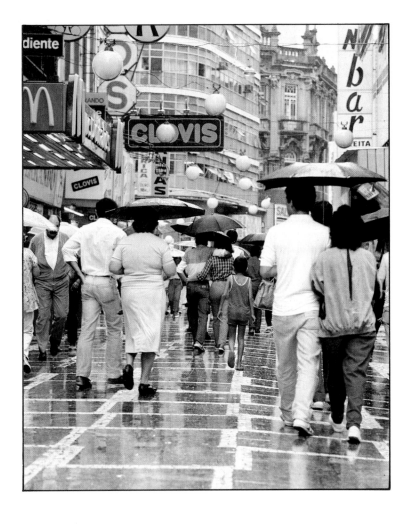

Before long, Carlos found himself downtown, surrounded by tall buildings. A thick haze of afternoon pollution hung in the air, along with the heavy smell of exhaust fumes coming from the many Brazilian cars that ran on pure alcohol. People rushed by him in all directions. But nobody noticed him. Nobody cared.

The sky had turned dark and cloudy. Then big drops of rain began to fall. Carlos sat down on the steps of an old cathedral. The wind made goose bumps appear up and down his arms. He shivered in the gray, lonely afternoon.

After a while the rain stopped. As Carlos got up off the steps, he noticed the aroma of something delicious waft through the air. Hunger pangs began to pierce his stomach. But there would be nothing delicious for him to eat.

He walked down a dark, narrow alley until he came to the back door of a restaurant. Several trash bags filled with old food scraps lay outside. Carlos brushed away the flies, then pulled out an apple core and a boiled pig's ear that had been used to spice a black-bean dish called **feijoada**. He ate quickly and hurried back to the street. The scraps of food tasted awful, but at least they filled his stomach.

The sun set and the evening air grew chilly. Carlos looked for an old newspaper to use as a blanket. After walking around for a while, he decided to spend that night on the front steps of a bank. He climbed away from the wind and lay down. He tried to cover himself with the newspaper he had found. As he lay there shivering on the hard steps, large tears rolled down his cheeks.

Finally, the noise of the city traffic stopped. But Carlos was still awake and shivering. The cold cut right through his bones. Suddenly he heard something different from the other night sounds. He strained to listen. It sounded almost like singing! It sounded like the kind of music Tia Noeme sang at the boys' camp.

Carlos sat upright, tossing the newspaper aside. He ran to the corner and looked down the desolate street. In the middle of the block, across the avenue, he saw a small, brightly lit building between two skyscrapers. Carlos hurried across the street. As he approached the door he thought he heard the same song Tia Noeme had sung before. Or could it be?

Carlos peeked through the crack between the open doors. A group of children was singing, and there was Tia Noeme leading them! Carlos was filled with happiness. Eagerly, he pulled the door wide open and joined the children in the very front row.

Carlos listened carefully as Tia Noeme told the children about the love of Jesus. When the meeting was over, Carlos hurried up to Tia Noeme. Her eyes sparkled with excitement when she recognized him.

"How did you get out of the boys' camp?" she asked.

Carlos told her all about it. Then he told her that Uncle Bento was dead. "I'm all alone now," he said.

"Well, you've come to the right place," replied Tia Noeme. "This is a place for kids just like you. We have food and beds for street kids without homes or families of their own. We want you to stay with us. You belong here, Carlos!"

Carlos' smile had never been brighter or bigger. "And I want to give my life to Jesus!" he exclaimed.

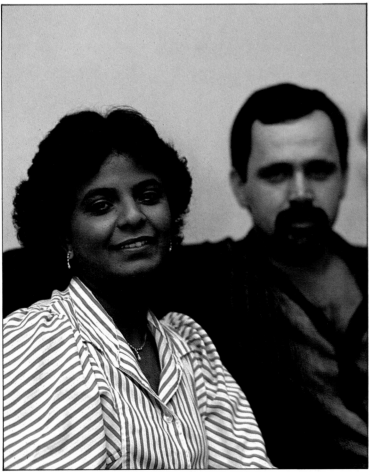

One morning Tia Noeme greeted Carlos with more excitement than usual. "Come into my office," she said. "There are some people here who want to meet you."

Carlos came in and saw a kind-looking man and a woman sitting on the couch. "Carlos," Tia Noeme began, "this is Reinaldo and Maria Souza. They have no children, and have come here because they would like to adopt a homeless boy to be their son. I have told them all about you."

Carlos looked at the man and woman. They were smiling at him. Their eyes were full of hope. For a moment Carlos remembered all the times he had cried because he had wished he had at least one parent. He looked at Tia Noeme, then at the Souzas once more.

Carlos spent the afternoon with Reinaldo and Maria, talking and walking around town. They bought Carlos a big hamburger and the best milkshake he had ever had. Then they returned to Tia Noeme. Carlos told her he had made up his mind. He wanted to go home with them.

"Great!" was all Reinaldo could say. Tears of happiness streamed down Maria's face. She hugged Carlos. And he hugged her back.

Tia Noeme was not in doubt about where Carlos belonged. "I know you'll be very happy," she said, wiping tears from her eyes.

Carlos climbed into the back seat of the Souzas' car once more. As they rode along, Maria told him all about their own lives. Carlos had never met anyone in his life who seemed more loving or caring.

They continued to drive on and on, out of the city of São Paulo and into the country. At last, Carlos drifted off to sleep.

When he woke up, they were pulling into a driveway. Carlos looked out the car window and saw a real house with a chimney and a garden and windows of glass! Once inside, Maria showed him his very own room.

"We want you to feel right at home,

25

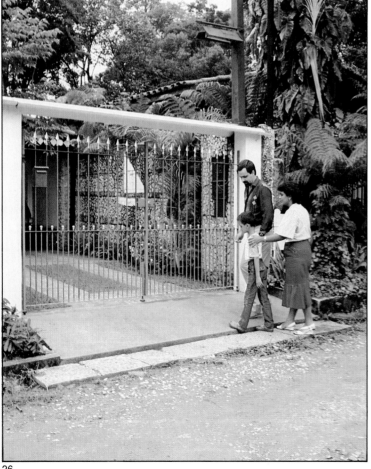

Carlos. Everything in this room is yours." Maria leaned down and kissed him on the cheek. "I'm so glad you're here," she whispered.

During supper, Reinaldo told Carlos, "You can begin going to school after summer vacation. You will start in March."

The next morning Carlos was served a big breakfast. It was the first time in his life he had ever had so much at one time. There was coffee mixed with hot milk, French bread, papaya slices, ham, mozzarella cheese, and Carlos' favorite—thick slabs of a thick, dark paste made from the tasty guava fruit. He had never tasted anything so wonderful.

Just as he was finishing, the doorbell rang. Maria opened the door, and Carlos saw a group of boys in shorts and soccer shoes. One of them was holding a leather ball.

"We heard there was a new kid living here," said the tallest boy. "Can he play with us?"

Carlos' eyes lit up like fireworks. Like most Brazilian boys, he loved soccer. He had played it often in the favela, using a wadded-up grocery sack for a ball.

Once on the field, Carlos kicked the ball right past his opponents and into the goal.

"Hurray, Carlos!" shouted his new friends.

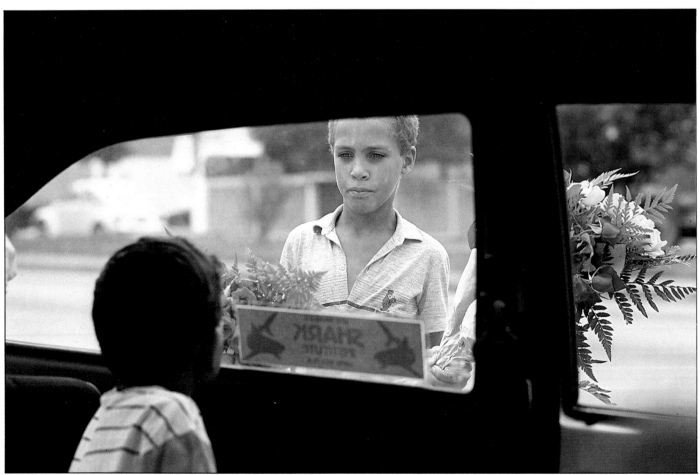

The following day was Sunday. "Carlos! Acorda! Wake up!"

Carlos sat up with a shock. For a moment he thought he was back in the boys' camp. But when he saw Reinaldo, a smile of relief crossed his face.

Reinaldo said, "We're going to Sunday school today. You'll make even more friends and learn about how God answers prayer."

"Oh, I already know all about that!" Carlos replied. "You are the answer to my prayers!"

A few weeks later Reinaldo asked if Carlos would like to drive into the city with him for the day.

"Yeah!" Carlos shouted. He loved riding in the car almost as much as he loved to play soccer.

At the end of the day, as they were leaving São Paulo and heading home again, Reinaldo stopped the car at a red light. A sad-looking boy approached their car, holding several bunches of roses. Carlos' heart sank. The boy was wearing a torn shirt and had dirty hair. Angry drivers were yelling at him. Reinaldo gave the boy some money for the roses.

Carlos watched the boy head toward other cars. He knew what it felt like to sell roses in heavy traffic, to be hungry and homeless and afraid all the time.

"I wonder where that boy will sleep tonight," Carlos said to Reinaldo.

That night as Carlos lay in his clean, warm bed he remembered the boy selling flowers. "He is just like me," he thought. "But things have changed for me. Why, Lord, do some children have to suffer, while others have so much? Thank you for giving me a home and a mom and a dad. Give the boy with the flowers what he needs tonight, and let him hear about Jesus, too."

The light of the moon bathed the countryside in a gentle glow as the cool rain started to fall. Inside the cozy house, Carlos fell sound asleep.

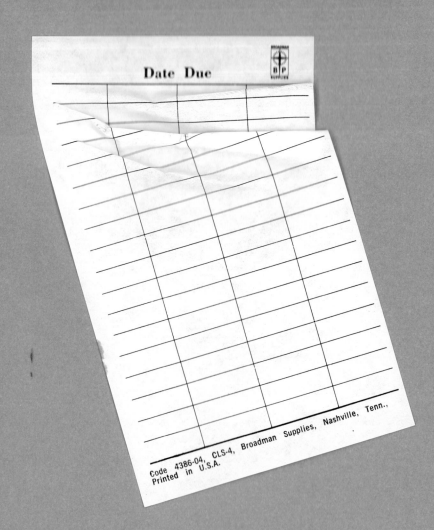

Date Due

Code 4386-04, CLS-4, Broadman Supplies, Nashville, Tenn.,
Printed in U.S.A.